MARGARET OF CASTELLO: UNWANTED ONE

For St. Mary School Library. Peace to all who read this book.

by
Sister Mary Pelagia Litkowski, O.P.

*Best wishes
Sister M. Pelagia Litkowski O.P.*

Illustrated by

**Students of
Mrs. Annette Plamondon
Teacher of Grade 2 at
St. Francis Elementary School
in Traverse City, MI**

Copyright © 1991 by
Sister Mary Pelagia Litkowski
All rights reserved, including the right of
reproduction in whole or part, in any form.

Published by

GROWTH UNLIMITED INC.
Dedicated to creating positive living concepts

**Art Fettig, President
31 East Avenue S., Battle Creek, Michigan 49017**

$5.95

Growth Unlimited books are available at quantity discounts with bulk purchase for educational, business or sales promotional use. For information, please contact Special Sales Dept., Growth Unlimited Inc., 31 East Ave. S., Battle Creek, MI 49017, (616) 965-2229 or 1-800-441-7676.

Manufactured in the United States of America

**Design, Layout and Typesetting
by**

350 Ward Ave., Suite 106
Honolulu, HI 96814
(808) 422-6825

Library of Congress Catalog Number
90-084543
Litkowski, Sister Mary Pelagia, O.P.
Margaret of Castello: Unwanted One
ISBN 0-916927-14-8

Dedication

For Estelle O'Leary, my elementary school teacher, who first awakened in my heart the desire to become a sister. She was the first to instill in me a joy in the art of writing. Also, in memory of Sister Eucharia Doris, O.P., my high school English teacher, recently gone Home to God, at age 98, who did so much to develop whatever writing talent God had given me and who fostered by prayer and example, this vocation to religious life.

Imprimatur

Given by
Patrick R. Cooney
Bishop of Gaylord
Thursday, July 5, 1990

Table of Contents

Dedication and Imprimatur . . . . *iii*
Preface . . . . *vi*
Introduction . . . . *vii*

1	Unwanted Child	1
2	Joyful Prisoner	9
3	Abandoned One	15
4	Unselfish Servant	21
5	Peaceful Prophet	27
6	Powerful Intercessor	33
7	Love's Recompense	39

Aftermath *42*
Prayer for the Canonization of
Blessed Margaret of Castello, O.P. *43*
Acknowledgements *48*
Bibliography *49*
Other Sources of Information About
Blessed Margaret *50*
Highlights in the Life of
Blessed Margaret of Castello *51*
Other Books by Sister *53*

Preface

This book would never have been written if the mother of Margaret of Castello had lived in the 1990's instead of the 1280's. She wanted to present her husband, one of Italy's foremost generals, with a son. When the child was born a girl, and a girl with major disabilities as well, the parents hid Margaret away, ignored her, and eventually abandoned her. With the high-tech tests we have for the unborn today, Margaret's mother might have gone to an abortion clinic.

Margaret of Castello, Unwanted One is the inspiring story of what a marvelous influence a disabled person can have and how God can use the unwanted to help meet the deepest wants of others.

Pope John Paul is canonizing new men and women saints several times a year because, as he puts it, "our world needs modern heroes and heroines and modern models." Margaret of Castello is not a modern heroine in the sense that the challenge of her life is perhaps the most serious challenge of our time. Never before, it seems, have so many unwanted children been conceived in our world.

The author of this book, Sister Mary Pelagia Litkowski, like Margaret of Castello a member of the Third Order of St. Dominic, taught me religion, reading, writing and 'rithmetic in 1935 and 1936. More than 50 years later, Sister Mary Pelagia is still teaching! This little book attests to it, and I am pleased to recommend it to readers young and older for the message it has for our modern age.

Kenneth J. Povish
Bishop of Lansing
April 13, 1990
(Feast of Blessed Margaret of Castello)

Introduction

Today, unborn children need an advocate.
Today, unwanted, abused, abandoned children need a defender.
Today, the aged, the homeless, the helpless, poor, imprisoned and the suffering need a patron.
Blessed Margaret of Castello is such an advocate, such a defender, such a patron. That is why I have chosen to write about her. Because of all her deformities and imperfections, she was herself unwanted, rejected and abandoned by her parents. She was familiar with the path of pain. She can identify with those who walk that path. Through her intercession their pain can be healed or relieved.
And what of those who caused that pain? Even to them Blessed Margaret can offer help. No one understood those who caused her suffering better than she herself did. By her loving forgiveness and understanding she was a living example of God's all-knowing, understanding, forgiving love.
Who, better than children, could illustrate the story of an unwanted child? I leave that question for the reader to answer.
Biblical quotes are from the **New American Bible**.

Bridget Mason

A daughter, not a son!

1

Unwanted Child

"...The Lord called me from birth, from my mother's womb. He gave me my name."

Isaiah 49:1

"Parisio is hoping that Lady Emilia will soon present him with a son."

"How will he feel if his hope is not realized? How will he feel if she presents him with a daughter?"

"Probably very much disappointed. But a beautiful daughter could bring into Metola a noble lord, a fearless and capable soldier like himself to protect and preserve their mighty fortress."

"Woe be to us if Parisio's hope is not realized! He's monster enough when things are going his way."

Such were the observations aired furtively about in the servants' quarters around the castle of Metola. Parisio was the powerful and wealthy Captain of the People, the Commander of the region of Trabaria in Italy, near Florence. The time was 1287 and everyone knew that his wife, the Lady Emilia, was about to give birth. With ill concealed joy Parisio looked forward to the birth of a son who would carry on the family name and even become the rich and powerful ruler of one of the Papal States.

"We must have not only one but two banquets in honor of our son," he said in glad anticipation, "one here for the servants and one at Mercatello for our friends."

"It will be something they will never forget," Emilia chimed in enthusiastically, "a double celebration, one in honor of our son's birth and one in honor of his baptism."

"Very clever, Emilia, very clever," Parisio had not thought of baptism for his son. "It would not be to my advantage if my enemies thought that the Captain of the People in a Papal State did not have his son baptised. Yes, we will have him baptised."

Not long after Parisio and lady Emilia had decided on two celebrations in honor of the birth of a son this news was noised about among the poorly fed servants of Metola. They always welcomed several days of feasting and fun which the birth of an heir to the Captain of the Castle would bring them.

Finally, Emilia's time came. But all was silent in the castle. Everyone wondered why no castle bell rang, why there was no banquet, no celebration . Soon the news was spread from one serf to another.

"Have you heard the terrible news? Have you heard why there is no banquet or celebration?"

"No, we haven't. Why? Aren't we going to have a celebration?"

"Lady Emilia has given birth to a girl."

"That would have been enough of a disappointment to Parisio. The girl is ugly, a dwarf, crippled and hunch-backed. Lady Emilia and Parisio are devastated. They have announced that the girl is very sick and may not live long. They are hiding her."

It was not long before the servants learned that the little girl was also blind. Parisio directed them to keep a strict silence about his crippled daughter. Fearing his displeasure, they obeyed. The woman who was commissioned to care for the child kept her hidden from visitors.

Padre Capellano, the pastor of the parish of Metola and chaplain of the Castle, did not fear Parisio. He reminded Parisio that, in accord with the ancient custom in Massa Trabaria, all babies must be baptised in the Cathedral

Church in Mercatello and that it was his duty to comply with this custom. Parisio stubbornly refused, until he was finally persuaded by Lady Emilia to give unwilling consent. Emilia's maid took the baby to Mercatello. Having been instructed by Emilia to make sure the child was not named Emilia, the maid had her named Margaret. Little did she realize what a prophetic significance this name would have in the life of this daughter of the Captain of the Castle of Metola and Lady Emilia.

In spite of her manifold deformities, Margaret soon began to show remarkable intelligence. Padre Capellano began to give her religious instructions and her nurse allowed her to leave her room and wander around the Castle at will. At first the inhabitants of the castle were stunned when they saw how ugly and repulsive Margaret's appearance was. But her pleasant and cheerful disposition soon won her the friendship and love of all who lived at Metola. Because of the hatred and abhorrence her parents had for their daughter, they forbade the nurse to permit Margaret to enter their living quarters.

Excited conversations among Margaret's friends were whispered in the halls of the Castle and other buildings of Metola and in the passageways of the fort:

"Can you imagine a blind five year old learning all our names and finding her way around without help?"

"It's almost unbelievable!"

"Padre Capellano says he is astonished at the remarkable understanding she has of God and His love for us. He says he has never taught anyone so intelligent."

"I love to see her coming. She is such a joyful, friendly little girl. Her visits bring sunshine into my life. They make my day."

"Parisio and Emilia aren't even giving themselves a chance to learn to know and love their daughter."

"My little Maria cries if Margaret ever misses visiting us. She asks where Margaret is and why she didn't come."

Padre Capellano tried his best to change Parisio and Emilia's attitude toward their daughter. They paid little attention to the stories he told them about her intelligence and about her happy relationship with the inhabitants of Metola. They would have nothing to do with her. Now and then visitors came to Metola. On these occasions Margaret was forbidden to leave her room. Once Margaret's nurse forgot to give Margaret the usual warning. One of the visiting ladies met Margaret on her way to the chapel to pray as was her custom. One of the servants who happened to be near enough to see and hear what happened could not wait to tell the others what she had seen and heard. In the privacy of their homes, soldiers and their wives, and other inhabitants of Metola spread the story.

"Margaret was on her way to the chapel when one of the visiting ladies came along. She began to talk to Margaret. I heard her ask what her mother's name is."

"Oh! Oh! Did she tell the lady?"

"She didn't have a chance. Margaret's nurse came running down the hall. She rudely pushed Margaret back toward her room. She told the lady that Margaret was sick and was supposed to stay in her room, and scolded her as if she had been very naughty."

Margaret's nurse lost no time in reporting the incident to Parisio and Lady Emilia. She made no secret of their reaction and of their plan to prevent the repetition of a like occurrence.

The corridors fairly buzzed with conversations about what might become of poor Margaret because of this incident.

"One of the visitors almost found out that Margaret is the daughter of Parisio and Emilia!"

"Really? How did it happen?"

"Margaret was on her way to the chapel where she goes everyday to pray. One of the visiting ladies met her. You know how friendly Margaret is. The lady asked her if she was blind and then asked her who her mother is."

"Horrors! Did the lady find out?"

"Just as Margaret was about to answer her, Nurse Lilia came running up to them and angrily pulled Margaret away. She told the lady Margaret was very sick and that she was told to stay in her room."

"I saw that happen. The way Lilia scolded her you would think she was a very bad, disobedient child."

"How did Margaret take that?"

"Like she always does. She was very sweet and told Lilia she was sorry. Then she quietly returned to her room."

"We're not going to see our little Margaret around any more."

"Why? Will she be kept locked up in her room?"

"No. Worse than that. Nurse Lilia told some of us that Parisio has had a little one room cell built next to our parish Church of St. Mary out there in the woods. They locked Margaret up in that cell. There is a window opening up into the church. She can hear the priest as he offers the Mass in church but the people in the church can't see her."

"The door into the cell was walled up so no one can go in and Margaret can't come out! The person who brings food to her through the window will be the only one to have any contact with her."

"I've never heard of anything so cruel!"

Shortly after this, in the home of the second knight in command of Metola, Leonardo di Peneto, a heated conversation took place between himself and his wife, Gemma:

"Oh, Leonardo, isn't there someone who can make Parisio change his mind? Poor, dear little child! How can a five-year-old child survive all alone in the woods? She'll freeze in that cold cell!"

"Everyone is angry about it. But I was the only one who wasn't afraid to try to dissuade him. It only made Parisio angrier."

"You were the *only* one who wasn't afraid to try?"

5

"The only one except Padre Capellano. As soon as he heard what had happened, he hurried to Parisio's quarters. I could hear them both yelling at each other."

"Our own kind and gentle Padre angry enough to yell?"

"Can you blame him? I could tell he was trying to get Parisio to give up his insane plan."

"Good for him!"

"That made Parisio angrier than ever. He threatened to do the Padre great physical harm."

"What happened then?"

"On his way out Padre Capellano fairly screamed, 'May the anger of God come down upon you both, Parisio and Emilia!'"

In the midst of this conversation, Leonardo and Lady Gemma heard a determined knock at their door. It was Padre Capellano. After the usual greetings, their conversation turned to little Margaret's plight.

"Father, excuse my tears. I think Margaret would be better off if she died. What a miserable life she will have in that cold cell in the woods!"

"Do not weep, Gemma. Margaret is putting into practice exactly what our Lord and His Church have taught us."

"How is she doing that, Father?"

"Jesus taught that the first and greatest Commandment is the love of God and that the second is like it, the love of neighbor. We know that at no time has Margaret ever broken either one of these commandments."

"But she is so young. She knows that she is not like other children. She knows that her parents hate her and are ashamed of her."

"Gemma and I are wondering how she can possibly refrain from becoming bitter and resentful."

"Father, if Margaret does avoid hatred and bitterness, she surely will lose her mind."

"My dear friends, have you ever stopped to think that we do not need a perfect body? We can love God and our neighbor even though deformed in any way. Margaret has a loving heart and remarkable intelligence. Isn't because of the grace God has given her?"

"But she is so young, Father. How can we expect her to act like a saint?"

"Gemma is right, Father, Margaret is too young. We cannot expect her to act like a saint."

"Isn't that what God wants us all to strive to become? I went to see how Margaret was doing in that cell. I was astounded when I saw how she reacted."

"Could it be anything but the sadness of a broken heart? You must have seen her crying as if her heart was breaking."

"Oh yes, Gemma, she was crying."

"What did I tell you, Father?"

"Like any child, she did feel the pain of her parents' hatred and cruelty. However, to my great surprise, I soon learned that her tears were tears of joy."

"Unbelievable! How could they be tears of joy?"

"That they were, Gemma. Margaret told me that at first she wondered why God had permitted this to happen to her. She asked Him. Suddenly she remembered how Jesus had suffered all for love of us. She was filled with peace at the thought of God's love for her. She thanked Him for allowing her to suffer rejection like He did and asked Him to give her the grace to accept her suffering and to increase her love for Him."

Padre Capellano's words left Leonardo and Gemma speechless. He left them to ponder in silence what he had told them.

Colleen McIntyre

In her one room cell near the church in the woods.

2

Joyful Prisoner

"Even now I find my joy in the suffering I endure for you."

Colossians 1:24

Margaret's friends really missed their happy visits with her when she lived in the Castle of Metola. They eagerly sought news of her from Padre Capellano, who visited her regularly. Her friends, Leonardo and Gemma, especially, were concerned. During one of their visits with Padre Capellano, they were amazed at the account their chaplain gave of Margaret's truly edifying and extraordinary understanding and acceptance of her suffering.

"Mark my words, dear friends, the fact that Margaret is cheerful and at peace is no sign that she is not suffering greatly."

"Then how can she be joyful, Father?"

"Gemma, do not forget that Margaret has learned much from her instructions about God. She understands that God is our Father. She knows that He loved us so much that He sent Jesus His Son to suffer and die on the cross for us so that we could live with Him forever in heaven."

"Gemma has heard that Margaret's mother visits once in awhile and spends the whole time cruelly bemoaning her misfortune at having given birth to such a disgracefully ugly and deformed child."

"How could that make her joyful, Father?"

"She knows that God created her soul in His own image and likeness and that it does not matter that she is physically deformed. This knowledge has filled her with joy. She is determined to love Him in return. In spite of her natural feelings which might cause her to return hate for hate, she is determined, by the grace of God, to love and forgive her parents. She often prays for that grace and recalls often the words of Jesus as He hung on the Cross, 'Father, forgive them, for they know not what they do.'"

"What marvels of grace God works in souls! Father, pray for me and Leonardo, that we, too, can learn to love God as Margaret does."

As Margaret grew older, it was her own prayers and the prayers of her friends that obtained for her the graces she needed. She was a normal human being subject to natural longings and inclinations. It was especially difficult for her to cope with these as she entered into adolescence. The fact that she could offer Holy Mass with the priest whenever it was offered in the little chapel, receive the Sacraments of Reconciliation and Holy Eucharist, and spend much time in prayer to Jesus in the Blessed Sacrament sustained her in these struggles. She also received much needed instruction and encouragement from Padre Capellano who visited her regularly.

Thirteen years passed by. Little did Margaret realize that her imprisonment at Metola would soon come to an abrupt end and that she would undergo greater trials than ever before.

Frederic of Montefeltro, one of the ablest generals of Italy, was beginning to invade Massa Trabaria. The watchman who saw flames and smoke from homes that had been set afire, informed Leonardo. He in turn gave the alarm and Parisio, as Captain, immediately began to insure the safety of the fort. He organized an army using serfs as soldiers. He ordered the young soldiers to take part in a counter attack. The older soldiers would see to the protection of the Castle.

Lady Emilia's maid learned that Parisio was sending her to Mercatello where she would be safer. It did not take the maid long to spread this news to other servants in the Castle. There was much whispering behind closed doors:

"Do you know that Parisio intends to send Lady Emilia to Mercatello where she'll be safer?"

"How did you learn that?"

"Lady Emilia's maid told me. She heard Parisio telling Lady Emilia to get ready immediately. She seemed very happy at the prospect of living at Mercatello."

"What will happen to Margaret?"

"Lady Emilia asked Parisio that very question. Parisio told her angrily that she'd have to take Margaret with her because she would be discovered by the enemy if they left her in the forest."

"How did Emilia take that?"

"She wondered how they would be able to hide Margaret at Mercatello. They would be entertaining many guests."

"Parisio didn't like that, did he?"

"Believe it or not! He reminded Lady Emilia that Mercatello has vaults in the basement of the palace where Margaret can be hidden."

"How cruel!"

"Lady Emilia mentioned that Margaret would want to attend Mass and receive the Sacraments. Then Parisio really blew up!"

"He's so afraid everyone would find out who she is if ever Margaret appeared in Church for Mass."

Early the next morning after the alarm had warned the inhabitants that Massa Trabaria was being invaded and that Mctola was in grave danger, Lady Emilia and Margaret, wearing a heavy veil, departed for Mercatello. They were accompanied by a group of servants. Margaret soon found herself locked in one of the vaults under the palace. The only furniture in the vault was an old wooden cot and bench. She was told that a meal would be brought to her twice a day. Only at those times was she to make known any of her wants. She was forbidden to call anyone or make noise of any kind.

The maid who brought Margaret's meals to her was appalled at the sight of Margaret's prison and did what she could to help Margaret. But there was not much she could say or do for her. She whispered to fellow servants what she saw or heard each time she brought Margaret her food.

"I could hardly believe what I saw when I brought Margaret her first meal! She is locked up in a dingy vault under the palace. There's nothing in it but an old bench and a hard little cot."

"And how is Margaret doing in that miserable prison?"

"Once I found her on her knees and she was crying. I asked her if there was anything I could do for her or bring to her."

"She stopped crying and smiled sweetly. She thanked me for bringing her food and said she didn't need anything just then."

"I told her how sorry we are that she is locked up down there away from everyone and that we wish we could help her."

"What did she say to that?"

"She admitted that it was hard for her to be cooped up down there. She said she misses hearing the beautiful sounds of nature which she enjoyed while in her little cell at Metola. But she assured me that she is at peace and happy and that we must not be sorry for her because God must have some reason for permitting her to suffer."

"I wonder how a person so young could take so much without bitterness. "

"She has told me that it is Jesus who has helped her to overcome temptations to bitterness."

"What kind of temptations has she had to face?"

"I asked her that and she said that she has not always understood why certain things have happened to her and that she was tempted at first to rebel. After praying about it she began to tell herself that she must realize all that her parents have had to undergo because of having a child like herself. She decided to show her love for God by loving them and accepting whatever God wills for her."

"What a wonderful example she is giving to us who don't have nearly as much to suffer as she has."

Long and arduous journey to Mercatello.

Colleen McIntyre

Who dares to take the alms that we hope to get?

3

Abandoned One

"Though my father and mother forsake me, yet will the Lord receive me."

Psalms 27:10

After months of fighting, Parisio, with the help of soldiers from neighboring states, succeeded in conquering Montefeltro and his army of invaders. On his return to Mercatello, Lady Emilia filled him in on all that had happened during his absence. She was most excited about the news which a group of pilgrims from Rome had brought with them. People in Castello were experiencing miraculous cures at the tomb of Fra Giacomo, a Franciscan Tertiary, who had recently died. She began to entertain the hope for a cure for Margaret. Parisio scoffed at the idea. After much persuasion, Emilia convinced him that they had nothing to lose by taking Margaret to the Shrine.

Almost overnight, Parisio and Emilia were on their way to Castello, leaving the servants to discuss among themselves, this unexpected occurrence in Margaret's life.

"You should have seen how happy Margaret was when Emilia told her they would take her to the tomb of Fra Giacomo to pray for her cure."

"You mean Parisio and Emilia are taking Margaret to Castello expecting her to be healed? I can't believe it!"

"I was just as surprised as you are."

"There must be some catch to it."

"They told Margaret that they intend to go to Confession and receive Holy Communion before asking for a miracle. That made her happier than ever."

"I'd like to see the day that Parisio goes to Confession and receives Holy Communion. That *would* be a miracle."

"Time will tell whether they keep their promise. Margaret has promised to pray for herself. But I know that when she prays for something, she asks God to give it to her *only* if it is His will."

"I wonder what will happen if her prayers aren't answered?"

"Only God knows what Parisio will do if she isn't cured. I only hope no more terrible things happen to her."

After a long and arduous journey on horseback, Parisio, Emilia and Margaret, with the escort of soldiers that accompanied them, finally reached the town of Citta di Castello. Emilia and Margaret rested comfortably at one of the best inns while Parisio went about the town seeking information about the Shrine of Fra Giacomo and the cures which had been obtained there. What he learned convinced him that the cures were genuine. He informed Emilia and Margaret that they would visit the shrine in the morning. Margaret could hardly contain her joy, especially because Parisio had made her believe that they would all go to Confession and receive Holy Communion.

With eager anticipation Margaret accompanied her parents to the shrine. In her prayers she asked God to cure her only if it were His holy will. She could not know that Parisio and Emilia had no intention of keeping their promise to receive the Sacraments. Neither could she know what they would do if she were not cured. Even Emilia did not know what Parisio was planning. When they realized that there was no change in Margaret's condition Parisio informed Emilia what they would do. Margaret would no longer be their problem. While she waited anxiously for them to join her after the Mass was ended and the worshippers left the shrine, they lost no time returning to the inn where they had spent the night. Without further delay they left the town. Long before Margaret began to realize that they had left without her, they were well on their way to Mercatello.

All day Margaret waited and prayed. She hoped that no mishap had befallen her parents. It came time for the sexton, a Franciscan lay-brother, to close the church for the night. With a few questions he learned that she was dwarf, twenty years old, and blind. She assured him that she did not mind waiting outside the church and that she expected her parents to come after her soon.

All night long Margaret sat on the church step, waiting. She was in a strange place. She dared not go into the unfamiliar street. Even though she had thought of this, she had no intention of absenting herself from the place she felt her parents would expect to find her on their return. She thought less of her own anxiety and fear than of their suffering when they returned and did not find her there. Morning came and her hopes began to fade. Beggars began to make their way towards the church, hoping for alms from people coming to worship. When they saw that a stranger had preceded them, they were very upset and wondered who would dare to encroach upon their territory.

"Who in the world is that ugly creature taking our place?"

"She can't be very poor. Look at the beautiful clothes she's wearing."

"Let's find out what she's doing here."

They approached Margaret and began to question her. They soon learned that she was waiting for her parents who had brought her to the shrine, hoping for a cure. They helped her find the inn where her parents had stayed the night before. The inn keeper informed them that Margaret's parents had left. Further investigation brought to light the fact that Parisio and Emilia had really left the city and taken the road to Mercatello. Margaret was finally convinced that her parents had abandoned her once and for all. She knew that she must now take care of herself.

During the weeks and months that followed, the beggars and street people overcame their repugnance towards Margaret's ugliness and did all they could to help her. They led her around until she could find her way by herself. They showed her where she could spend her nights, where she could find water, where to beg for food. She learned to love these friends, who were so kind to her as if they were her own brothers and sisters.

Autumn followed summer. Winter followed autumn and with it came cold nights and snow storms. During one of these more severe storms, at night, a friend of Margaret's found her crouching in a doorway. She was covered with snow and shivering with cold. Soon she and her friend found a stable and obtained permission from the owner to spend the night in it. What happened there gave the beggars much food for thought and conversation.

"I've been wondering how anyone could be as happy as Margaret after what her parents did to her."

"Do you know what she said to me when I said what I thought about parents who could be so brutal as to abandon their own child?"

"Oh, yes, I know. She always takes their part and says that they deserved to be relieved of the burden she had been to them. She said they had taken care of her for twenty years and that it is only right that she take care of herself now."

"I never hear her say anything bad about anybody and she always seems so happy."

"I asked her once how she could be so happy."

"What was her reason?"

"She said she always asks God to help her think the best about people and to love them as He does. That and God's love for her is what makes her so happy."

"When I took her to that stable, the night of that terrible snow storm, I thought she cried because of sleeping in an animal shelter. Well, I soon learned, to my surprise, that she was thrilled to think that God loved her so much that He let her find shelter in a stable just as Joseph and Mary found shelter in a stable the night that Jesus was born."

"Incredible!"

"She even convinced me that God loves me, too, no matter what I've done. I never thought that God cared a hoot about me. Now, I'm even thanking God for loving me, and telling Him I'm sorry for the bad things I've done."

"I used to think she was putting on. I didn't think anybody could be happy after what she had to suffer. I don't think so anymore. Just being with her makes me feel happy, too."

Audrey McDonnell

Margaret always makes me happy.

Jennifer Plamondon

Margaret's friends loved her more and more each day.

4

Unselfish Servant

"God is not unjust, He will not forget your work and the love you have shown Him by your service."

Hebrews 6:10

Beggars and street people were not the only ones who came to know Margaret. Soon, Margaret caught the attention of many citizens in Castello, especially the poor. She won their friendship and many families took turns offering her a home. She lived with each family as long as that family could afford to keep her. In spite of uncleanliness in the homes, inconveniences and lack of privacy, the love of these friends added much to Margaret's happiness. The loving gratitude with which she accepted the kindness of her friends dispelled any doubts which any may have entertained about the genuineness of her virtues. Her presence in these homes brought with it many blessings to her benefactors. They began to imitate her Christlikeness and they received unexpected material blessings, such as gifts, jobs, and job promotions.

Eventually Margaret's reputation reached the cloistered nuns of St. Margaret's Monastery. History does not specify the Order to which these nuns belonged. After some persuasion on the part of Margaret's friends, these nuns took the necessary steps, according to Church law, which resulted in their inviting and accepting her into their Community. Margaret's joy knew no bounds. She surprised the nuns by becoming a helpful member of their Community instead of a dependent one as some had feared. Her friends rejoiced with her and felt that at last she had found her niche in life. However, again Margaret's joy was short-lived. She was very different from the other members. As sometimes happens among very human beings, there were misunderstandings which could not be resolved. Margaret was dismissed from the Convent.

With a broken heart she took up her life again among the beggars and street people who had first befriended her. Again Margaret became a much discussed topic among these and other friends.

"When I heard that Margaret was dismissed from the Convent, I could scarcely believe it!"

"It's hard to believe, but it's true. I wonder whatever happened that made the nuns dismiss someone as good as Margaret is."

"The other day when I saw her, I asked her how come she wasn't in the Convent anymore."

"Did she tell you why?"

"She said she just did not measure up. The Sisters were kind and loving to her, but she just could not adapt herself to their way of life."

"When I asked her what she would do now, she said she trusts that God will take care of her."

"She told me that she doesn't think she is good enough to be a nun. I can't believe that. She is a living saint, if you ask me."

"We have invited her to live with us. We've told her she is good enough for us."

And so, Margaret was offered a home again. This did not mean that she was free from suffering. Only her friends who had known her still believed in her goodness. Many others, after hearing of her dismissal from the Convent, were a source of bitter heart break to her. Whispered gossip, malicious slurs, and unkind jeers, even from children, about the ex-nun who pretended to be a saint followed her where ever she went.

During this time in her life, Margaret continued her visits to the churches with which she had become familiar. She attended Mass daily at the Chiesa della Carita (the Church of Charity). The Dominican friars were in charge of this church. It was the headquarters for an order of lay women called the Order of Penance of St. Dominic. These women were called Mantellate because of the black cloak called a mantella which they wore. This Order was founded for older widows who wished to lead a religious life while living at home. These women learned from Margaret of her great desire to be a religious. The witness to Christ of her life convinced them that she was a worthy candidate for their Order, even though only in her twenties and single. They made this known to the Dominican friars and asked them to invite Margaret to join them. At first the friars hesitated to do this. After much persuasion on the part of the Mantellate, the Father Prior finally agreed to make an exception with regard to Margaret. He asked a group of women to make a thorough study of Margaret's life. This resulted in his giving his formal consent. She was instructed to present herself for admittance into the Order of Penance of St. Dominic.

Once more joy filled Margaret's heart. A beautiful ceremony was conducted in the Church of Charity. It was filled with Dominican Friars, Mantellate and Margaret's friends. She made her profession as a member of the Order of Penance of St. Dominic and promised to live according to the rule of that Order, as she had been instructed by members of the Order.

With joy Margaret entered upon her new ministry as a Mantellata. Stories of how she lived in action and spirit the charism of the Order of St. Dominic spread far and wide.

"Now that Margaret is a Mantellata, I've heard that she spends even more time in prayer than she ever did before."

"I've heard that, too. And, believe it or not, she recites the 150 Psalms of David, the Office of the Blessed Virgin and the Office of the Holy Cross from memory."

"Yes, she memorized those, I think, while she was in the convent, just by listening to the Sisters praying them."

"Surely the Holy Spirit helped her do that."

"How can she spend so much time in prayer and still do all the good that she is doing as a Mantellata?"

"God is really doing it through her, is all I can say. She thinks so much about God and talks to Him and about Him so much, people can't help thinking about God when they see her."

"She even does the penances prescribed for members of the Order of St. Dominic. You'd think that all she suffers because of her blindness and lameness would be penance enough for her."

"She has often mentioned that she is so grateful to God for His boundless love and for sending His only Son Jesus for our salvation. She is so grateful to God for being allowed to serve Him in His people as a Mantellata."

"Yes, I've heard that. She thinks that whatever penances she can offer to God are little enough to show how thankful she is for all the suffering Jesus did for us."

"She takes to heart everything she hears the Friars preach in their conferences and homilies as if they were speaking directly to her."

"She certainly is living religious life even though she doesn't live in a convent."

"What kind of penances does Margaret perform?"

"Well, I know the Offrenduccios and the Macretis, those two high society families that live in a grand house they call Domus Pacis (House of Peace). Margaret has been living with them ever since she became a Mantellata. Lady Beatrice, Messer Offrenduccio's wife, told me about some of Margaret's penances."

"Like what?"

"She spends much of her time in prayer and meditation. Early in the morning when she hears the monastery bell ring for the friars to rise for morning prayers, she goes to the Church of Charity for daily celebration of the Holy Eucharist."

"Besides all the time she spends in prayer and meditation, she is forever doing something for someone who needs help. She knows where to get food for the hungry, clothes for the poor, or medicine for the sick. She comforts people who are sad and lonely."

"She can even talk sinners into changing their ways and turning back to God."

"She is so concerned about the sufferings of others that she forgets she has any."

"I've never heard of anyone whose love for people could match hers; especially those who are suffering."

"Once I was very discouraged. So many bad things had happened in my life I wondered how much longer I could carry on. When I learned how Margaret accepted her great sufferings, I was ashamed and asked God to help me take mine cheerfully."

"I love to hear Margaret talk about God and His love for us. She seems especially thrilled with the thought that Jesus came as a little child and that He was cared for by His mother Mary and foster father Joseph."

"Oh, yes. I know how much she loves St. Joseph. If you are ever in a hurry, don't mention St. Joseph! She will talk about him as long as you will listen! On and on! There is no end to the wonderful things she can say about St. Joseph."

"Did she ever tell you how fast you can obtain help from God if you ask St. Joseph to pray for you, especially if you need help to provide for your family? I myself have received help soon after praying to St. Joseph."

Bridget Williams

Praying joyfully with the Mantellate.

5

Peaceful Prophet

"The spirits of the prophets are under the prophets' control, since God is a God, not of confusion, but of peace."
I Corinthians 14:32

Margaret's life as a Mantellata won for her widespread admiration and love. Whoever came to know her felt that there lived in their midst a truly courageous lover of God and His people, one imbued with faith and confidence in God's loving care. All was sunshine at last in Margaret's life. And then—

"It is really wonderful that the Offrenduccios have invited Margaret to stay with them."

"She will have a comfortable home at last. They are a very well-to-do family and can afford to offer her a well-furnished apartment."

"Yes. I've heard of Margaret's living in the high society Offrenduccio's House of Peace. But it's not so peaceful since she began to live with them."

"How could that be? Margaret always brings peace with her."

"You know that there is another family living with the Offrenduccio's, don't you?"

"Yes. Lady Beatrice's sister, Ysachina, her husband, Messer Macreti and their daughter Francesca live with them."

"What does that have to do with Margaret?"

"You know that Ysachina and Messer Macreti are not at all religious. Francesca (they call her Ceccha) hasn't received any religious instruction. She is sixteen years old and doesn't know her prayers. She hasn't been to Confession since she made her First Holy Communion. Margaret has been instructing her ever since she learned this about Ceccha."

"How has that disturbed the peace of the House?"

"Her parents weren't too disturbed about that but something else has aroused their anger."

"What in the world could that be?"

"Margaret and Cecca have become close friends. Ceccha has admired Margaret so much, and has been greatly edified by her Christlike example and her joy in the service of God and His people. She wants to become a Mantellata, too."

"Oh, oh! I can see trouble brewing!"

"You're right there. The Macretis have no intention of allowing their Ceccha to become a Mantellata. They've already spotted a rich, respectable and handsome young man who they hope will choose to make her his wife."

"How do you know all this?"

"I heard from one of the ladies who was visiting the Macretis that Margaret asked Messer Macreti if he would permit Ceccha to become a Mantellata. This surprised and angered him and Ysachina. After they refused her request, Margaret told them that Ceccha and her mother would soon become Mantellate. When she said this there was a chorus of loud laughing. Everyone knows that Ysachina hardly ever goes to church and that she is very worldly."

"Time will tell whether this will happen. Who knows? It would not be the first time something happened that Margaret had foretold."

As all her friends knew, Margaret's prophecies did come true. Two which she made while living with the Offrenduccios were no exception. Not long after Margaret's prediction that Lady Ysachina and Ceccha would become Mantellate, Messer Macreti died of a sudden illness. Ysachina, in her sorrow, turned to God for consolation. She and her daughter then sought admittance into the Order of Penance of St. Dominic.

Another prophecy which Margaret made while with the Offrenduccio family surprised everyone. Messer Offrenduccio's son was caught up in the midst of dissension between two political parties. They were the Neri, who were in control of the government of Citta di Castello, and the Bianchi, who were determined to overthrow the Neri. Messer Offrenduccio's son was suspected of plotting against the Neri and arrested. If found guilty he would suffer a heavy fine and cruel penalties. He and his family were in danger of being banished from the State.

Beatrice knew that Margaret was always ready to come to the aid of anyone in distress. She confided her fears to Margaret, who, after turning to God in prayer, assured her that her son would be freed and his family would not be banished. Beatrice found it hard to believe this. Her doubts vanished when her son was released and no penalty was inflicted on him or the family.

The more Margaret's friends heard of her selfless love and concern for the sufferings of God's people, and of the help she brought to those in need, the more they loved her. The more blessings they received from God in answer to her prayers, the more they sought her help. Consequently they shared with their friends things in her life that might interest them.

"Have you heard that our little Margaret is not living with the Offrenduccio's any more?"

"Yes, I've heard. I'm wondering where she will be living now."

"The noble, Venturino invited her to come to live in his rich palace when he heard that the Offrenduccio household was broken up after Messer Macreti died."

"We were very happy for Margaret when we heard this."

"Did you know that Margaret felt uncomfortable in her luxurious room and asked Lord Venturino to give her a little room in the attic of their home?"

"That sounds just like Margaret. Did he let her move to the attic?"

"He did after Lady Gregoria, his wife, told him how one day she heard Margaret discussing with their boys what they had learned in school that day. They were reciting lessons that they had in logic, geometry, Latin, music and astronomy. Whenever they made a mistake, Margaret corrected them. They knew that Margaret could not have this knowledge unless God had put it into her mind directly."

"Margaret has been busier than ever since moving into the Venturino home."

"What could she possibly be doing now more than she had already done before?"

"When Margaret heard of the dreadful conditions in the city prison and how the prisoners were suffering, she immediately began to ask God to make it possible to help them. Lady Gregoria herself told me this. She had been wishing she could help but did not ask Lord Venturino because she was afraid she might expose him and their children to the diseases that so many of the prisoners have. She is a Mantellata, you know."

"How was Margaret's prayer answered?"

"She told Lord Venturino that she had heard about the terrible conditions in the prison. She asked if he could get the government to do something about it. He told her he had tried, but that nothing had been done because the only kind of men who could be hired as jailers were the very kind who would only make the conditions worse."

"Did Margaret say anything to that?"

"She didn't have a chance because Lord Venturino guessed that she wanted to visit the prisoners and minister to them. He gave her and Lady Gregoria permission to do this."

"Glory be to God! I always knew Lord Venturino was a true Christian."

"I've heard that the Lady Gregoria and Margaret have helped the prisoners in other ways besides bringing them food, clothing and medicine. They have reminded the prisoners that they are human beings created by God and that He loves them no matter what. Prisoners who had stopped believing in God, have begun to believe in Him again."

Max Janis

I love Margaret. She's my best friend.

Audrey McDonnell

Margaret! Margaret! Come down! The house is on fire!

6

Powerful Intercessor

"The Lord has heard my plea; the Lord has accepted my prayer."

Psalms 6:10

The esteem with which Margaret was held by the people of Citta-di-Castello increased from day to day. This was due not only to her loving ministry to anyone in need. Reports of miracles obtained through her ministry spread far and wide until it became impossible for her to avoid publicity, which she would have liked to do. Even people with little or no faith had to admit that Margaret must be one of God's specially chosen ones, very close to Him.

"Lady Gregoria, when you first told me about your friend Margaret, I was very skeptical, and wondered how anyone so ugly, so handicapped, could do all she has been doing."

"We were sure my little niece would not last through the night. The doctors had done all they could. They told us there was no hope. She kept on getting worse. That night we stood around her bed waiting for her to breathe her last."

"Where did you say Margaret was at this time?"

"She was kneeling in the hall, just outside the door where my niece lay dying. She was praying so fervently she did not even notice us coming in. This did not seem unusual to me. Margaret would pray for any sick person like that. But she was even more greatly concerned because she is my niece's godmother."

"Did Margaret come in and touch her?"

"No. In the middle of the night, after the monastery bell rang, my niece woke up, smiled at us and told us that God had cured her in answer to Margaret's prayers. She turned over and went to sleep. She has been perfectly healthy ever since."

"If there was any doubt in my mind about Margaret, it is not there any more."

"Were you there when Venturino's house caught fire?"

"Indeed I was! I helped carry buckets of water to try to put out the fire. It spread so rapidly, that we were getting nowhere."

"I hear that Margaret put the fire out. How did she do that?"

"The Senior Warden was telling Lady Gregoria how sorry he was, but that her home was doomed. He said we could not save it and that it was a good thing no one was in the house."

"Margaret was, wasn't she?"

"Lady Gregoria had forgotten that Margaret was still in her room in the attic. She started to run into the house after her, but the men stopped her. Lady Gregoria began to scream for Margaret to hurry down the stairs and out of the house. Then something happened I'll never forget."

"I'm all ears."

"Margaret came quietly to the top of the stairs and called to Lady Gregoria, telling her not to be afraid and to trust in God. She rolled her cloak into a round ball and threw it down to Lady Gregoria. She told her to throw it into the fire. Lady Gregoria did that and immediately the flames were extinguished."

"Margaret loves God and people so much that even her own sufferings make her happy. She considers it real joy to have sufferings to offer to God."

"I know. Some people think that she doesn't suffer from her deformities, and those who know forget it because she is always so cheerful."

"Venturella forgot that when she went to Margaret, all upset because her doctor told her she might become blind because of a tumor in her eye."

"Yes. Can you imagine Venturella telling Margaret she thinks God would be cruel to let her become blind?"

"How did Margaret answer that complaint?"

"She tried to make Venturella see that God permits such things for our own spiritual good, that He wants her to come closer to Him."

"Did it do any good?"

"No. When Margaret saw that she couldn't convince Venturella, she held out her hand and asked Venturella to touch her eye with it. As soon as Margaret's hand touched the eye, the tumor disappeared and Venturella could see perfectly."

"How do you suppose Venturella felt when she remembered that Margaret herself was blind even from birth?"

"I don't know. I know if I were Venturella, I really would have been embarrassed."

"Margaret obtains miracles for everyone. Even the prisoners in the city jail believe she is a saint. There was one who hated God so much and blasphemed so harshly that no one dared to come near him. Then one day he saw Margaret kneeling, not on the floor, but up in the air! He knew she was praying and looked as if she could see God. I'm sure you've guessed the rest of the story. That prisoner stopped blaspheming and asked Margaret to pray for him."

"Have you noticed that Margaret is getting weak lately? She seems to be almost worn out. Young as she is, I'm afraid it won't be long before God calls her Home."

"I was talking to one of the Dominican friars the other day. He says that her love of God is so great that her soul is struggling to be separated from her body, so she can be with God in Heaven. Margaret told him she can see Jesus between the Consecration and the Communion of the Mass."

"Did she offer him any kind of proof that she really does see Jesus?"

"The friar tested her with all kinds of questions. Before he was finished he was sure that she really does see Jesus at that time of the Mass even though she sees nothing or no one else."

"I'm beginning to think that we won't have Margaret with us much longer. She herself seems to know this and looks happier than ever."

Mark Oleson

The prisoners were in need of faith in God's love for them.

Carolyn Schilling

Margaret was happy to join the Sisters.

Suddenly the girl jumped up and cried, "I'm cured!"

7

Love's Recompense

"The Lord will be your light forever; your God shall be your glory."

Isaiah 60:19

Margaret's friends, who believed her time in this world was about to end, were right. Consequently, they were not surprised when they heard that she had requested the Dominican friars to administer the Sacrament of Annointing to her. Like a flash of lightning the message that Margaret was dying reached every home in the town, especially the homes of the Mantellate. They filled the house of Venturino, tearfully waiting for word about Margaret. Some of them were able to enter the room where Margaret was receiving her Eucharistic Lord for the last time on this earth and the grace of the Sacrament of Annointing.

On April 13, 1320, the second Sunday after Easter, Margaret died as she had lived, filled with the love of God and the joy of having lived during her whole life in accordance with His will.

The Mantellate took charge of preparing Margaret's body for the funeral. Because Margaret, as a Mantellata, had spent her life in voluntary poverty, preparations for the funeral were the same as funeral preparations for the poor. There was no embalming, no coffin. Her body was carried in procession on a wooden frame toward the Chiesa del Carita.

Margaret's friends from far and near were already assembled in the church. It was filled to overflowing and surrounded by an enormous crowd.

After the funeral service, the friars were in for a surprise. Never had they experienced the protests of a determined crowd of people like these who demanded that Margaret be buried in the church and not in the cloister where they were about to take her.

Even Margaret's friends who were part of this demonstration could not believe that these ordinary people would dare to oppose the friars so boldly.

"They actually barred the doorway so that the procession couldn't possibly leave the church to go to the cloister."

"I know. I was there. I was protesting, too. Every one knows that our little Margaret is a saint."

"It was pretty hard to hear what Father Prior was trying to say. When he finally got everybody's attention, what we heard him say made sense. It is the church that proclaims whether a person is a saint after proper investigation of the person's life."

"But everyone felt that there was no need for investigation. We could never count all the miracles that Margaret's prayers have obtained for us."

"Wish I'd been there. How did all this turn out?"

"Margaret was buried in the church. But it wasn't so much the people's protests that made the Prior change his mind. It was a real miracle that happened while the people were protesting."

"Yes, yes! Go on!"

"A man and woman brought their little girl into the church. She was blind, mute and crippled. They carried her to the stand on which Margaret's body had been laid. There they prayed hard."

"Then what happened?"

"Everyone stopped talking. They began to pray to Margaret for the little girl. Suddenly Margaret's left arm rose into the air and touched the little girl."

"What happened then?"

"The girl suddenly jumped up, threw her arms around her mother and cried, "I'm cured! I'm cured! Margaret's prayers have cured me!"

"Again Margaret proved that we are right about her."

"And so the Prior gave in. Margaret was buried in the church, and everyone gave praise to God for hearing our dear little Margaret's prayers."

Margaret's friends visited her tomb day after day. They received countless blessings and more than 250 miracles after asking her intercession. She became known throughout Italy until attention was diverted from her by the Black Death, a plague which killed millions of people throughout Europe like wars among European countries which also took millions of lives.

Eventually interest in Margaret revived. On June 9, 1558, her body was exhumed and found perfectly incorrupt. Since it had not been embalmed this was another proof of her holiness.

In 1600 Pope Clement VIII authorized an investigation of Margaret's life. He died before he could read the report which had been submitted to him. Pope Paul V who succeeded him studied the report. He beatified Margaret on October 19, 1609. April 13 was named as her feast day.

So Margaret of Castello, blind, crippled, dwarfed, hunchbacked and ugly, unwanted, hated and abandoned by those who gave her life, reached the heights of holiness—of love of God and neighbor.

Aftermath

Today, after more than 650 years Blessed Margaret's body is still perfectly incorrupt. It lies in state in the Church of St. Domenico at Citta-di-Castello, Italy.

Today, Margaret's friends and devotees are praying and working for her canonization. It is their hope that she will be proclaimed soon, the patron saint of the UNWANTED, the advocate of today's victims of abortion, child abuse and euthanasia.

Today, members of the Pro-Life Movement and the American Life League look to her for the inspiration and spiritual help they need in their battle against the enemies of life.

Blessed Margaret's Cause can be furthered by ordering materials from or reporting favors received through her intercession to:

Fr. David Wright, O.P.
Coordinator of Blessed Margaret Cause
Priory of St. Dominic—St. Thomas
7200 West Division Street
River Forest, IL 60305

Gary Crum, Director
Castello Institute
188 Onville Road
Stafford, VA 22554

Fr. Cataude, O.P., Director
Blessed Margaret of Castello Crusade
Holy Name Church
701 E. Gaul Street
Philadelphia, PA 19125

Mrs. Judie Brown, President
American Life League
National Headquarters
188 Onville Road
Stafford, VA 22554

Prayer for the Canonization of Blessed Margaret of Castello, O.P.

O God, you illuminated the mind and inflamed the heart of your blind servant Margaret. Grant to her prayers the favor we now ask, and hasten the cause for her canonization. We ask this through Christ, Our Lord. Amen Blessed Margaret of Castello, pray for us.

Nine-Day Prayer Imploring Blessed Margaret of Castello's Intercession

1st Day—

O Blessed Margaret of Castello, in embracing your life just as it was, you gave us an example of resignation to the Will of God. In so accepting God's Will, you knew that you would grow in virtue, glorify God, save your own soul and help the souls of your neighbors. Obtain for me the grace to recognize the Will of God in all that may happen to me in my life and so resign myself to it. Obtain for me also the special favor which I ask through your intercession with God.

Let us pray

O God, by whose Will the blessed virgin, Margaret, was blind from birth, that the eyes of her mind being inwardly enlightened she might think without ceasing on you alone; be the light of our eyes, that we may be able to flee the shadows of this world, and reach the home of neverending light. We ask this through Christ, Our Lord. Amen.

Jesus, Mary, Joseph glorify your servant blessed Margaret by granting the favor we so ardently desire. This we ask in humble submission to God's Will, for His honor and glory and the salvation of souls.

N.B. Say One Our Father, Hail Mary and Glory be to the Father after each day's prayer.

2nd Day—

O Blessed Margaret of Castello, in reflecting so deeply upon the sufferings and death of our Crucified Lord, you learned courage and gained the grace to bear your own afflictions. Obtain for me the grace and courage that I so urgently need so as to be able to bear my infirmities and endure my afflictions in union with our Suffering Savior. Obtain for me also the special favor which I now ask through your intercession with God.

Let us pray: O God, etc.

3rd Day—

O Blessed Margaret of Castello, your love for Jesus in the Blessed Sacrament was intense and enduring. It was here in intimacy with the Divine Presence that you found the spiritual strength to accept sufferings, to be cheerful, patient, and kindly toward others. Obtain for me the grace that I may draw from this same source as from an inexhaustible font, the strength whereby I may be kind and understanding of everyone despite whatever pain or discomfort may come my way. Obtain for me also the special favor which I now ask through your intercession with God.

Let us pray: O God, etc.

4th Day—

O Blessed Margaret of Castello, you unceasingly turned to God in prayer with confidence and trust in His fatherly love. It was only through continual prayer that you were enabled to accept your misfortunes, to be serene, patient, and at peace. Obtain for me the grace to persevere in my prayer, confident that God will give me the help to carry whatever cross comes into my life. Obtain for me also the special favor which I now ask through your intercession with God.
Let us pray: O God, etc.

5th Day—

O Blessed Margaret of Castello, in imitation of the Child Jesus, Who was subject to Mary and Joseph, you obeyed your father and mother, overlooking their unnatural harshness. Obtain for me that same attitude of obedience toward all those who have legitimate authority over me, most especially toward the Holy Roman Catholic Church. Obtain for me also the special favor which I now ask through your intercession with God.
Let us pray: O God, etc.

6th Day—

O Blessed Margaret of Castello, your miseries taught you better than any teacher the weakness and frailty of human nature. Obtain for me the grace to recognize my human limitations and to acknowledge my utter dependence upon God. Acquire for me that abandonment which leaves me completely at the mercy of God to do with me whatsoever He wills. Obtain for me also the special favor which I now ask through your intercession with God.
Let us pray: O God, etc.

7th Day—

O Blessed Margaret of Castello, you could have so easily become discouraged and bitter; but, instead, you fixed your eyes on the Suffering Christ and there you learned from Him the redemptive value of suffering—how to offer your pains and aches, in reparation for sin and for the salvation of souls. Obtain for me the grace to learn how to endure my sufferings with patience. Obtain for me also the special favor which I now ask through your intercession with God.
Let us pray: O God, etc.

8th Day—

O Blessed Margaret of Castello, how it must have hurt when your parents abandoned you! Yet you learned from this that all earthly love and affection, even for those who are closest, must be sanctified. And so, despite everything, you continued to love your parents—but now you loved them in God. Obtain for me the grace that I might see all my human loves and affections in their proper perspective—in God and for God. Obtain for me also the special favor which I now ask through your intercession with God.
Let us pray: O God, etc.

9th Day—

O Blessed Margaret of Castello, through your suffering and misfortune, you became sensitive to the sufferings of others. Your heart reached out to everyone in trouble—the sick, the hungry, the dying, prisoners. Obtain for me the grace to recognize Jesus in everyone with whom I come into contact, especially in the poor, the wretched, the unwanted! Obtain for me also the special favor which I now ask through your intercession with God.
Let us pray: O God, etc

Sister Mary Pelagia Litkowski, O.P.

Prayer

O my God, I thank You for having given Blessed Margaret of Castello to the world as an example of the degree of holiness that can be attained by anyone who truly loves You regardless of physical abnormalities. In today's perverted culture, Margaret would have, most likely, never been born; death through abortion being preferable to life, especially life in an ugly distorted, twisted body. But Your ways are not the world's ways...and so it was Your Will that Margaret would be born into the world with just such a malformed body. It is Your way that uses our weakness to give testimony to Your power. Margaret was born blind, so as to see You more clearly; a cripple, so as to lean on You completely; dwarfed in physical posture, so as to become a giant in the spiritual order; hunchbacked, so as to more perfectly resemble the twisted, crucified body of Your Son. Margaret's whole life was an enactment of the words expressed by Paul: "So I shall be very happy to make my weaknesses my special boast so that the power of Christ may stay over me and that is why I am content with my weaknesses, and with insults, hardships, persecutions and the agonies I go through for Christ's sake. For it is when I am weak that I am strong." (2 Cor. 12:10)

I beseech You, O God, to grant, through the intercession of Blessed Margaret of Castello, that all the handicapped...and who among us is not?...all the rejected, all the **unwanted** of this world may make their weaknesses their own special boast so that Your power may stay over them now and forever. Amen. Blessed Margaret of Castello, pray for us!
(3 Our Fathers and 3 Hail Marys)

Imprimatur: (for above prayer)
Thomas J. McDonough, D.D.
Archbishop of Louisville
5 December 1980

Acknowledgements

To all my relatives, friends and benefactors who prayed for God's blessing and the guidance of the Holy Spirit on my writing, I wish to express my sincere and heartfelt gratitude. Special thanks, also, are due to:

Sister Carmelita Murphy, O.P., Prioress General of the Grand Rapids Dominicans, for her kind encouragement, support and permission.

Sister Jean Milhaupt, O.P., Professor of English at Aquinas College, Grand Rapids, Michigan for reading and critiquing the manuscript.

Sister Malvena Nadon, O.P., who spent many hours listening, encouraging, advising and challenging, patiently and kindly.

My niece, Marlette Reibel, and her husband, Lee Reibel, whose word processor produced the final typewritten manuscript, saving me many hours of precious time.

Bibliography

Bonniwell, O.P., Fr. Wm. R. *The Life of Blessed Margaret of Castello (1287—1320)* Madison, Wisconsin 53711, Idea, Inc. 1988.

Crader, Margaret. *Patron of the Persevering.* Catholic Digest, January, 1990.

Engel, Randy. *Blessed Margaret of Castello: A Good Patron for the Universal Pro-Life Apostolate.* Stafford, VA, Castello Institute of Stafford, 1978.

Literature from:

American Life League
National Headquarters
P.O. Box 1350
Stafford, VA 22554
Mrs. Judie Brown, President

Blessed Margaret of Castello Crusade
National Headquarters
Holy Name of Jesus Church
701 E. Gaul St.
Philadelphia, PA 19125
Fr. Cataude, O.P., Director

Blessed Margaret of Castello Crusade
Priory of St. Dominic/St. Thomas
7200 N. Division St.
River Forest, IL 60305
Fr. David Write, O.P., Coord.
for Blessed Margaret's Cause in the U.S.

Castello Institute of Stafford
188 Onville Rd.
Stafford, VA 22554
Gary Crum, Director

Other Sources of Information About Blessed Margaret

General Postulator
Generalate of Dominicans
Santa Sabina on the Aventine
Rome, Italy

Dominican Sisters
School for the Blind
Cita di Castello
Italy

(The incorrupt body of Blessed Margaret is enshrined in the chapel of the School for the Blind.)

Sister Mary Pelagia Litkowski, O.P.

Highlights in the life of Blessed Margaret of Castello:

1287 Margaret is born at Metola, Italy.

1320 April 13 — Margaret dies at Castello, Italy.

1558 Margaret's body is exhumed and found perfectly incorrupt.

1601 Margaret's cause is formalized by the Dominican Order.

1609 October 19 — Margaret is beatified by Pope Paul VI and April 13 is designated as her Feast Day.

Jenna Denoyer

Young soldiers guarded the fort.